Dedicated to Tyler, Grant & Madison.

Once there was a number 1 'twas all alone in this land.

1

Off he went upon a quest,
to find One to hold his hand.

2

He came across the number Two -- said, "surely I can't look like you?"

"...For, you are curved, as you can see, have you seen another 1 like me?"

Two said to One - "no, not at all..."

"...But number 3's just down the hall!.. Perhaps she's seen a One like you?" (Now number One knew what to do).

5

One walked along 'till he met Three,
then said, "have you seen One like me?"

The 3 then said, "I'm sorry dear, but you're the only One I've seen, I fear."

7

"But don't give up, or feel too down --
or let your face wear such a frown."

"For, what you search, I'm sure you'll find --
What may seem lost, will soon be found."

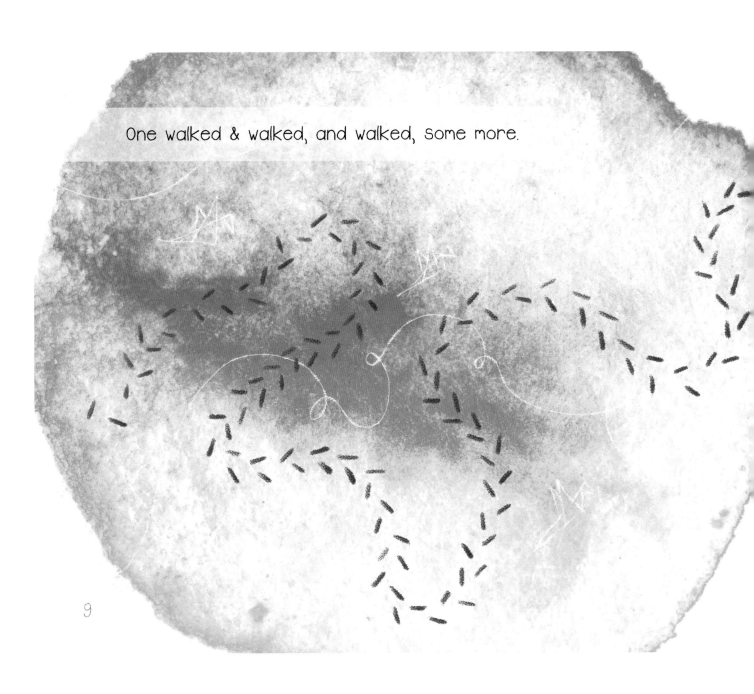

One walked & walked, and walked, some more.

9

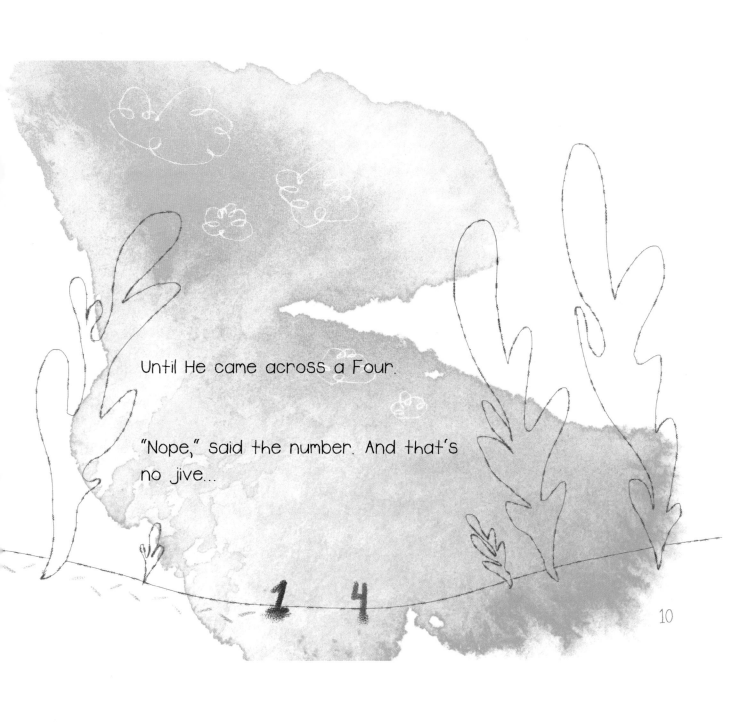

Until He came across a Four.

"Nope," said the number. And that's no jive...

The number Five said "No, not here.
But resourceful is the 6 I hear."

Six hadn't any help for One.

But this Quest he'd only just begun.

He would not stop till he'd reach the peaks of Heaven...

15

And thus, he came across a 7.

The Seven was wise and his knowledge was great.

He said, "your answer will lie within the 8."

18

One took this advice, and to Eight he did run --
as he thought to himself, this is really no fun.

19

This is taking too long & who ever knew, how hard it might
be to find someone like you...

When the One met with Eight, he began to look sad,
so the 8 said to One, "why the glum look -- that's bad?"

When he told her his story she understood fine.

"Though I'm sorry that I cannot help," she then said, "don't forget there is always the 9."

Off he went to meet Nine trying to maintain his hope.
And with a small smile, made best efforts to cope.

When the One met with Nine, know what happened then?...
The number Nine said, "you are in luck my friend!"

"I have seen One just like you! He lies within Ten."

26

The One was aghast, as he thought how profound...
that One looks just like me -- next to something so round!

Alas, the One had found a friend, had found him in the number 10.

He realized that there were others he had not seen --
think of couples 11, 12, 13, 14 and 15!

And then he thought, could it be true?...
Perhaps combined with number 2?

If coupled then, or placed between...
how large they'd grow as he'd just seen...

There was 28...45...14...53..21..16...73...187..2134...

Oh to see such a sight, made him all warm inside, all the friends he had met while searching in stride. How nice it does feel -- very settled, like home. My hope for all others?... should 'One' never feel alone.

Oh, Oh how many numbers.

May you find your number too.

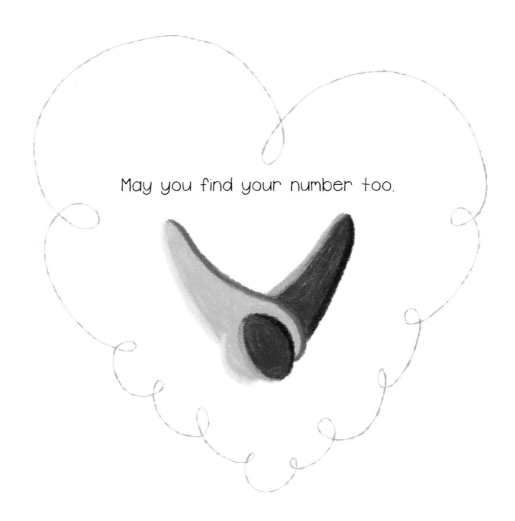

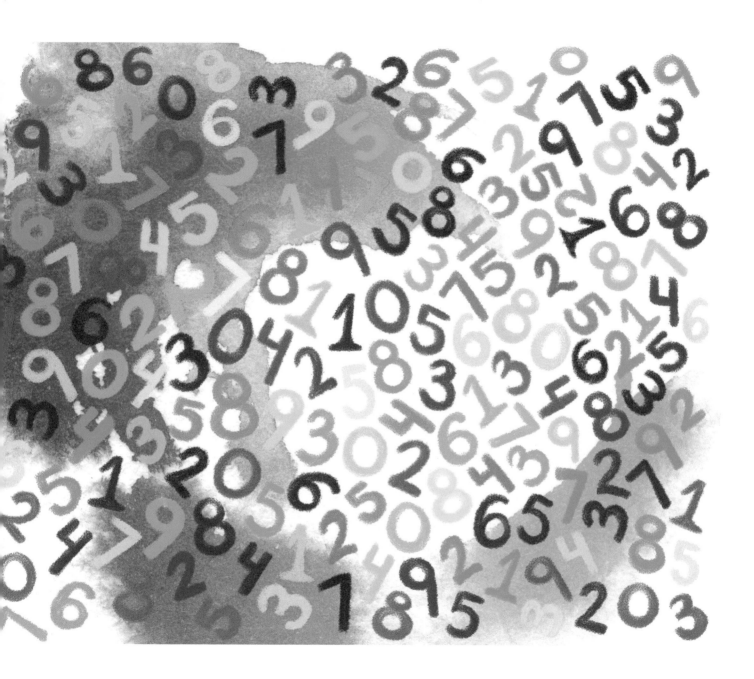

Made in the USA
Monee, IL
21 July 2020